This book belongs to

. . . .

Front endpapers by Selin Apaydın aged 8 (left) and Hasan Oğuz Kullelioğlu aged 8 (right)
Back endpapers by Siyabend Atlı aged 8 (left) and Selin Apaydın aged 8 (right)

Thank you to the children from Özel Bahçeşehir İlköğretim Okulu
who contributed pictures for the endpapers—K.P

For Maxwell and Giaan—V.T.
For James Watt who gave me my first freelance job—K.P.

OXFORD
UNIVERSITY PRESS

Great Clarendon Street, Oxford OX2 6DP

Oxford University Press is a department of the University of Oxford.
It furthers the University's objective of excellence in research, scholarship,
and education by publishing worldwide in

Oxford New York

Auckland Cape Town Dar es Salaam Hong Kong Karachi
Kuala Lumpur Madrid Melbourne Mexico City Nairobi
New Delhi Shanghai Taipei Toronto

With offices in
Argentina Austria Brazil Chile Czech Republic France Greece
Guatemala Hungary Italy Japan Poland Portugal Singapore
South Korea Switzerland Thailand Turkey Ukraine Vietnam

British Library Cataloguing in Publication Data available

First published in paperback in 2014
ISBN: 978-0-19-273602-4 (paperback)
ISBN: 978-0-19-273603-1 (paperback with audio CD)

2 4 6 8 10 9 7 5 3 1

Printed in Singapore

Paper used in the production of this book is a natural, recyclable product made
from wood grown in sustainable forests. The manufacturing process conforms
to the environmental regulations of the country of origin

Valerie Thomas and Korky Paul

Winnie's Pirate Adventure

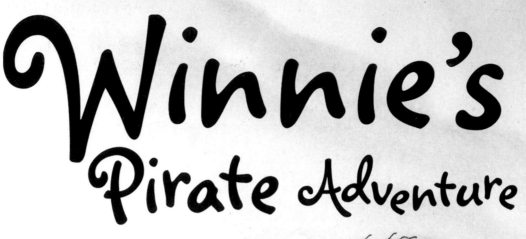

OXFORD
UNIVERSITY PRESS

Winnie the Witch and her big black cat
Wilbur were getting ready for a party.
It was a fancy dress party to celebrate
Cousin Cuthbert's birthday.

'What will we wear, Wilbur?' asked Winnie.
'We'll have to think about that.'

Winnie thought about it.

Cinderella?
No.

A bear?
No.

The Queen
of Hearts?
No, no!

Then Winnie had
a fantastic idea.

She waved her
magic wand,
shouted,
Abracadabra!

And there she was, wearing a pirate costume.
Wilbur was in a parrot suit.

Winnie was pleased.
'We look fantastic!' she said.

Wilbur was embarrassed.

'We look ridiculous,'
he thought.

Winnie jumped onto her broomstick,
Wilbur jumped onto her shoulder,
and they flew off to the party.

There were some wonderful costumes at the party.

Fairies, clowns, a lion, a princess, some spacemen and *lots* of pirates.

Happy Birthday, Cuthbert!

The other pirates admired Winnie's parrot.
Wilbur flapped his wings.

'All we need now is a treasure map,' one pirate said.
'I found a treasure map in my pocket,'
said another pirate.
'So all we need now is a ship.'

'I can do that,' said Winnie.
She waved her magic wand,
shouted,

Abracadabra!

And there was a pirate ship,
at the bottom of
Cuthbert's garden.

'Hurrah!'
shouted the pirates.
They climbed aboard
and sailed away.

'Yo-ho-ho!' shouted Winnie's pirates. 'Being a pirate is fun!'

They climbed up the masts.
They danced the hornpipe.
They walked the plank,
until Winnie fell in.

Luckily she could swim.

Wilbur climbed up to the crow's nest for a sleep,
but there was a crow inside.

'**Caw!**' said the crow.
She didn't want to share with a parrot.

Winnie's pirates got out the treasure map.
There were islands all around their ship.
Which one was the treasure island?

But then they saw an island
that looked exactly like the one
on the treasure map.

Winnie and her pirates splashed ashore.
They climbed to the top of a hill and
looked down.

There was another band of pirates digging up the treasure.
They had swords and daggers, cutlasses and blunderbusses.

They looked **fierce.**

'Will we stay and fight?' asked Winnie. 'Or go home?'

Winnie's pirates shouted . . .

'GO HOME!'

The real pirates looked up
and saw Winnie's pirates.

They ran back to their ship
with their swords and daggers,
their cutlasses and blunderbusses . . .

and sailed away.

Winnie's pirates were very surprised.

'Hurrah!' they shouted.
'We are fierce pirates!'

They ran down to the hole
in the sand and started digging.

It was hard work.

But at last they dug out the treasure chest.

Winnie lifted up the lid. The chest was empty.
'Shiver me timbers!' shouted Winnie's pirates.

'We've been hornswoggled!'

But Wilbur saw something
shining in the sand.

What was it?

He started to dig
and dig.

Out came a big shiny box.
And inside the box were lots
and lots of shiny tins . . . of sardines!

'Meeee-yo-ho-ho!'
Wilbur was delighted. He loved sardines.

Winnie's pirates were not delighted.

But Winnie had a
wonderful idea.

She waved her wand,
shouted,
Abracadabra!

And the
treasure
chest was full
of shiny treasure.

Now Winnie's pirates
were delighted.
They carried the treasure
and Wilbur's sardines
back to the ship.

It was time to go home, but there was
no wind to blow their ship home again.

'I can fix that,' Winnie said.
She waved her magic wand,
and shouted, *Abracadabra!*

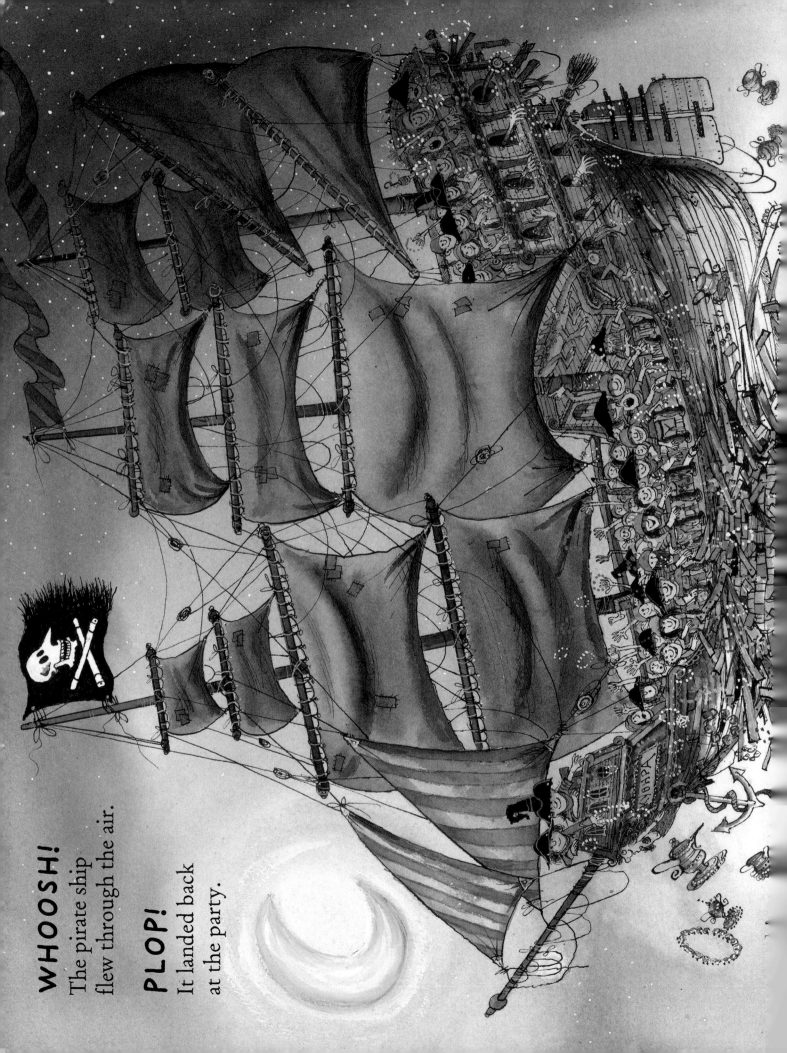

WHOOSH!
The pirate ship
flew through the air.

PLOP!
It landed back
at the party.

Winnie's pirates shared
the treasure with Cousin
Cuthbert and his friends.
They were delighted, too.

Wilbur didn't share his sardines.

'Being a pirate is fun, Wilbur,'
Winnie said. 'But being a witch
is much more fun.'

'*Purr, purr, purr*,'
said Wilbur.

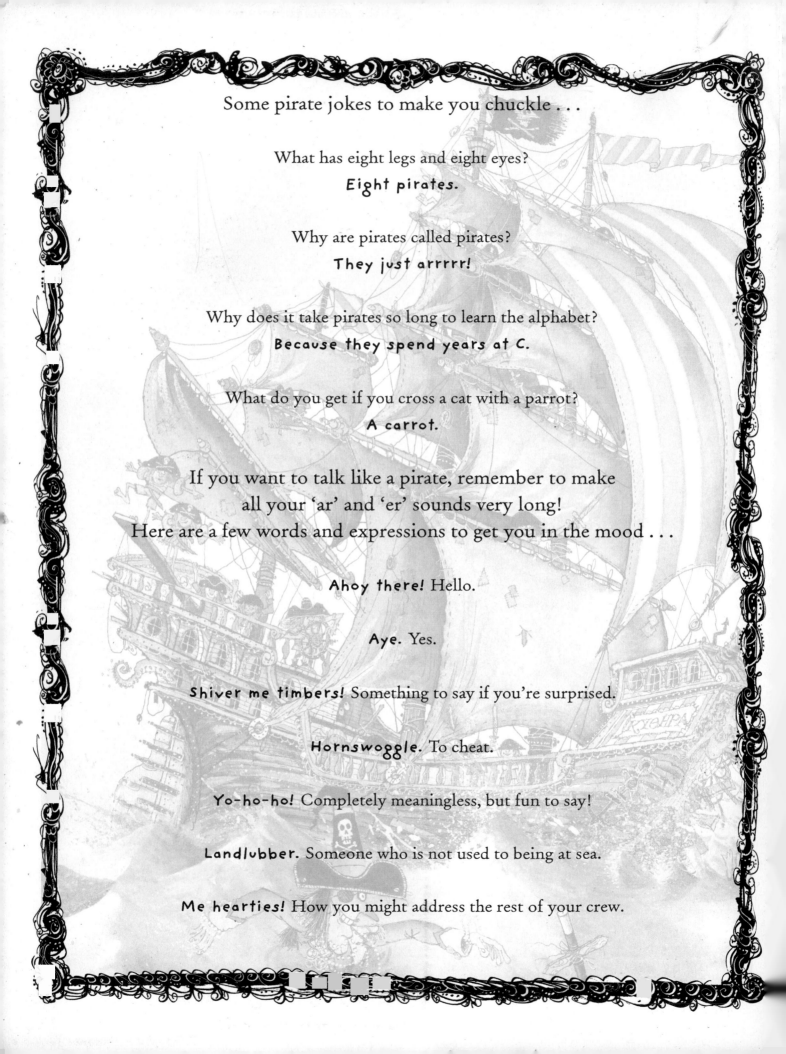

Some pirate jokes to make you chuckle . . .

What has eight legs and eight eyes?
Eight pirates.

Why are pirates called pirates?
They just arrrrr!

Why does it take pirates so long to learn the alphabet?
Because they spend years at C.

What do you get if you cross a cat with a parrot?
A carrot.

If you want to talk like a pirate, remember to make
all your 'ar' and 'er' sounds very long!
Here are a few words and expressions to get you in the mood . . .

Ahoy there! Hello.

Aye. Yes.

Shiver me timbers! Something to say if you're surprised.

Hornswoggle. To cheat.

Yo-ho-ho! Completely meaningless, but fun to say!

Landlubber. Someone who is not used to being at sea.

Me hearties! How you might address the rest of your crew.